For Craig and Honey.
You make me happy and glad every day. xx H.S.

tiger tales

an imprint of ME Media, LLC

5 River Road, Suite 128, Wilton, CT 06897

Published in the United States 2012

Originally published in Great Britain 2011

by HarperCollins Children's Books

a division of HarperCollins Publishers Ltd.

Text and illustrations copyright © 2011 Holly Surplice

CIP data is available

ISBN-13: 978-1-58925-112-0

ISBN-10: 1-58925-112-1

Printed in China

LPP 0112

For more insight and activities, visit us at www.tigertalesbooks.com

ABOUT A
BEAR

by Holly Surplice

tiger tales

A bear can be happy.

A bear can be sad.

A bear can be bored.

And a bear can be glad.

A bear can be puzzled

by a curious find.

And sometimes a bear has to scratch his behind!

A bear can be hungry,
and sniff out a treat.

And
no bear
can
resist
something
sticky
and
sweet.

A bear can be silly

and possibly slip.

But luckily a bear

makes a very good ship!

A bear can get sleepy

and need a bear hug.

Then cuddle up tight,
as snug as a bug.